Keeping Warm in Winter

by Susan M. Bauer

Strategy Focus

How do some animals survive during the cold winter months? As you read, pause from time to time to **summarize** what you have learned.

HOUGHTON MIFFLIN   BOSTON

Key Vocabulary

cache hidden supply

fashion make

harsh cruel; severe

harvesting gathering plants to eat later

migration movement to a different place

storehouse place where supplies are stored

survival ability to stay alive

Word Teaser

When it's time for a winter vacation
Some birds start a southern _____.

The ground is buried under two feet of snow. The lakes are covered with ice. People are bundled up in coats and mittens and scarves, if they're outside. Most are cozy and warm inside their homes.

But what about animals? How do they make it through a long, cold winter?

Some animals head south for the winter. They make a yearly migration to warmer areas where they can find food. Other animals go into a long, deep sleep for the winter.

But many animals stay around, and stay active, all winter. They must be well prepared to make sure of their survival. Staying alive is hard work.

Putting on a Winter Coat

Deer are used to harsh and difficult winters. Their winter coat helps them keep warm in the coldest weather. The coat is made of hair, not fur. Each hair is hollow, like a tiny drinking straw. The hair holds warm air inside. This gives the deer an extra layer of warmth, like the lining in your own winter jacket.

Weasels dress in a smart way all year round. In summer, they have brown fur coats. These coats match the ground and trees. In the cold of winter, their coats turn white to match the snow. This helps keep weasels safe, since their enemies have trouble seeing them.

Some weasels have another trick, too. When the rest of their coat turns white, their tail stays dark. If a hungry enemy does spot the weasel, it mistakes the black tail for the weasel's face. When the enemy tries to attack the weasel head-on, the weasel escapes in the other direction!

Snowshoe hares grow special coats of winter fur on their feet. This extra inch of fur helps them keep warm.

The snowshoe hare's fur helps in another way, too. It keeps hares from sliding in the snow and ice. For hares, slipping could be a matter of life or death. They spend a lot of time running from hungry foxes!

Food and Shelter

In the summer and early fall, the red fox begins harvesting nuts, fruits, and other foods. By winter, the fox's cache may contain everything from crickets to banana peels.

Usually, this storehouse of food is enough to see the fox through a long winter. But if a fox runs out of food, it can always hunt for more. Foxes are excellent winter hunters. They can hear even the tiniest sound from animals hidden below the snow. If a rabbit scratches its ear or a mouse nibbles on food, the fox knows where to dig and find its next meal.

Foxes have an easy time when it comes to shelter, too. Most animals fashion a burrow or nest below the earth or away from the wind. Foxes don't go to all this trouble. They just curl up on a bed of snow. They wrap up in their warm, furry tails and take a nap.

The next time you run inside to escape the winter wind, think of all the animals out in the cold. Each one is coping in its own special way.

Putting Words to Work

1. List three things you depend on for **survival**.

2. How does **migration** help some animals?

3. Describe the weather during a **harsh** winter.

4. Complete the following sentence:
   In the red fox's **cache**, there were _____ for_____.

5. **PARTNER ACTIVITY:** Think of a word you learned in the text. Explain its meaning to your partner and give an example.

Answer to Word Teaser
migration